D1575412

Because of You

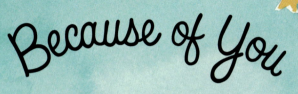

Because of You

A Book of Kindness

B. G. Hennessy

illustrated by

Hiroe Nakata

CANDLEWICK PRESS

Each time a child is born,
the world changes.

When you were born,
there was a new person
for your family to love
and care for.

And because of you,
there is one more person
who can love and care
for others.

Because of you,
there is one more person
who will grow and learn

and one more person
who can teach others.

Because of you,
there is one more person
to share with.

And there is one more person
who can share feelings and ideas,
as well as things.

Because of you,
there is one more person
who needs help

and one more person
who can help others.

When you help,
care, share, and listen,
you are being kind.

When two people help, care,
share, and listen to each other,
they are friends.

When people from
different countries
help, care, share, and
listen to one another,

it is called peace.

Even something as big
and important as peace
begins with something
small and precious.

It might begin . . .

because of you.

For my parents
B. G. H.

For children of the past, present, and future
H. N.

Text copyright © 2005 by B. G. Hennessy
Illustrations copyright © 2005 by Hiroe Nakata

First edition in this format 2011

The Library of Congress has cataloged the original hardcover edition as follows:

Hennessy, B. G. (Barbara G.)
Because of you / B. G. Hennessy ;
illustrated by Hiroe Nakata. —1st ed.
p. cm.
Summary: Tells how every single person helps make the world
a kinder and more peaceful place.
ISBN 978-0-7636-1926-8 (hardcover)
[1. Kindness—Fiction. 2. Conduct of life—Fiction.]
I. Nakata, Hiroe, ill. II. Title.
PZ7.H3914Be 2005
[E]—dc22   2004045168

ISBN 978-0-7636-3879-5 (midi hardcover)

11 12 13 14 15 16 CCP 10 9 8 7 6 5 4 3 2 1

Printed in Shenzhen, Guangdong, China

This book was typeset in Calligraphic 810.
The illustrations were done in watercolor and ink.

Candlewick Press
99 Dover Street
Somerville, Massachusetts 02144

visit us at www.candlewick.com